ELLIOT STANTON

Can It Still Just Be Me?

More Poetic Observations On Modern Life

To all those who have supported me on my literary journey.

Contents

SUNDAY MORNING

Sunday morning and with no plans for the day,
I'm happy just to lie here and while the hours away.

Clouds are dissipating, leaving clear blue skies above,
Two birds on a telephone wire preen each other; true love.

The distant rumble of traffic can be heard above their tweeting,
Two women up the road laugh in a ceremonial greeting.

A lawnmower starts up and stops almost straight away,
No doubt it's gone over the cable, causing a substantial delay.

An aeroplane crosses the sky leaving a vapour trail behind
Holidaymakers off to who knows where; their intention to unwind.

Through the open window, a soft breeze caresses my face,
I appreciate this peaceful quiet in this calm, relaxed place.

It's nine o' clock, and the house is beginning to stir.
Someone is walking about, and things are about to occur.

A floorboard creaks, and I hear a cough and a sneeze,
A sudden strong gust ousts the former gentle breeze.

The white noise of a hairdryer destroys the once peaceful morn,
A car alarm is triggered, provoking a piercing horn.

The television is switched on, and voices have been raised,
So much for the tranquillity that I so recently praised.

The buzz of the hairdryer is replaced by the vacuum cleaner,
All this sudden racket has done nothing for my demeanour.

Its time to get up and prepare for the day ahead,
Gone is the calm of Sunday morning, peacefully resting in my bed.

* * *

RHETORICAL MISCHIEF

Don't ask me a rhetorical question,
Because I'll answer it whether you like it or not.
I enjoy releasing the pedant inside me,
To keep my silence, I simply cannot.

'How long is a piece of string?'
It's two-foot, six inches, give or take.
The look I get back is one of confusion.
But, I answered the question, for heaven's sake.

'Ah, how can I be so stupid?'
You refuse to use knowledge and common sense.
Your idiotic question just proved that point.
However, it's not much of a defence.

'Are you trying to be funny?'
No, it just comes naturally to me.
I could tell you a joke to make you laugh,
But you probably won't just to spite me.

'Why do I keep making the same mistake?'
I'll refer you to my previous remark.
Or it could be due to a neurological deficit,
I mean, you're hardly the brightest spark.

If you think I'm being conceited,
And I'm behaving like a wise guy,
These are all questions I've asked myself,
My intelligence and wit, I belie.

* * *

CLICHÉD COLOUR COMMENTARY

Not every piece of skill is unbelievable.
Not every mistake is a disaster.
Not every great goal can be Goal of the Season.
Not every record book needs to be rewritten.
Not every converted penalty is perfect.
Not every missed one is shocking.
Not every mistimed tackle is heinous.
Not every injury is career-ending.
Not every win catapults a team to the title.
Not every defeat will dooms them to relegation.
Not every drag back is a Cruyff turn.
Not every dinked spot-kick is a Panenka.
Not every goal can win you a match.
Not every miss will lose you one either.
Not every Brazilian is a skilful wizard.
Not every Swede is cool and calm.
Not every Cup Final is a stunning showcase.
Not every six-pointer produces a win.

Not every line of commentary is eagerly accepted.
Not every silence is universally welcomed.
Clichéd colour is part of a commentator's armoury.
But sometimes black and white are all we need to see.

* * *

A BLANK SCREEN

The house is empty, and I have time to myself,
A mug of tea stands, steaming to my right.
I stretch my arms and adjust my keyboard,
In front of me, a blank screen of solid white.

I want to start writing my novel; I do,
But I don't have a clue where to start.
It has spent weeks swirling around my mind,
I know the whole story now, off by heart.

The plot is there; a crime has been committed,
And the accused stands alone in the dock.
The jury's sworn in, and the trial can begin,
This is no time for writer's block.

My fingers are poised, desperate to press,
On the keys to begin my literary journey.
But my brain's not playing ball today.
Leaving a speechless prosecuting attorney.

The scene is set, the characters in place,
And the charges have all been read out.
But a wave of inertia has engulfed the court,
Threatening to make the case a washout.

The draw of Facebook and YouTube is immense,
And only a little click or two away.
But no, I must resist their enticing charms,
And stay focused. I *won't* be led astray!

The brightness of the screen induces a headache,
And I'm desperately willing my story to appear.
Just a paragraph, a sentence; even a word or two,
Would start me off; I wish this blockage would clear.

I suppose I could start my tale from the middle,
And work on the start on another day?
At least I'd be able to get some work done,
Yes, I'll do that and begin without further delay.

My fingers have been hovering over my keyboard,
For ten whole minutes without any joy.
The words remain locked away in my brain,
When they should be spilling out in convoy.

My phone pings, and a message appears,
It's one of my fellow writer friends.
'How're you doing? Have you written much today?
I've written 3000 words. My creativity never ends.'

I've written four words (and then deleted three),
'The' is the only one that remains on the page.
Perhaps the silence of this room doesn't sit well with me.
Wisdom and intrigue have deserted this old sage.

Sure, when I'm at work or driving in my car,
Dialogue and plot come to me with ease.
They have me clamouring for a pencil or my phone,
To note down my thoughts before my mind can freeze.

Right, I'll give it an hour; maybe my brain will thaw,
And my words will begin to slowly drip.
Otherwise, I fear I'll get lost in YouTube again,
Then there's no chance of overcoming this blip.

So, I've watched an hour of cats playing the piano,
And even though the felines have been impressive,
I've finished the session with a single, solitary 'the'.
My total word count today is by no means excessive.

* * *

STOP, SLEEP, GO

For precisely 27 seconds, I have a little quiet time for myself,
Before I need to wake up to continue my morning task.
But as soon I shut my eyes and drift into blissful solitude,
The moment ends no time for my mind to relax and bask.

I've done this same thing dozens of times, maybe more.
And I know exactly when real life has to convene.
Before I continue my bleary-eyed journey into work,
As the traffic lights turn from red to amber, to green.

* * *

TOO MUCH CHINESE... AGAIN!

'We've ordered too much food as usual,'
I moaned, slumping back in my seat.
Once more, overdoing the Chinese again,
'We didn't need to order six types of meat.'

Following mixed hors d'oeuvres and a couple of soups,
And, of course, crispy aromatic duck,
Why the hell did we think it a good idea,
To order the other half, was it just for luck?

Shredded chilli beef and chicken balls,
Were next to be ordered in haste.
But adding char sui pork and Kung Po beef,
Our confidence was slightly misplaced.

There were sides of chow mein and two types of rice,
We weren't thinking of our welfare.
Chinese vegetables and a plate of seaweed on top,
Left us on the brink of needing healthcare.

Once the plates and dishes were taken away,
The mess left behind was quite frightening.
Dismissing the stains of sweet hoisin sauce,
The desire for dessert was heightening.

The choice was toffee apple or banana,
So, naturally, we decided to have both.
But that tipped me over the edge; I was sick,
And swore, never again, I promise... on oath.

* * *

MOBILE PRISON

Like an ankle tag but attached to your hand,
It's silently taking your freedom away.
It pumps largely irrelevant information into you,
Without even having a comforting word to say.

It's a drug, and you're hooked for life,
The only option is to turn off your phone.
But the pain of suffering technical cold turkey,
Is something that not many have known.

The most addictive social narcotic is Facebook,
Can any adult confidently disagree?
How we love to snoop on our friend's lives,
And for their every interaction, we oversee.

Who's talking about us, and indeed, who's not?
It can play terribly on one's addicted mind.
Because it's far worse *not* to be talked about,
Than to be the subject of gossip, however unkind.

Some become voyeurs; the watchers; the worriers,
The ones that sit and wait to be offended.
But there are more proactive individuals,
Who seek attention wherever it is extended.

Whether we are the detonator of the bomb,
Or the one who's caught explosion,
The lure of social media in every waking hour
Causes our normal life severe erosion.

They can be very tough to ignore—
That ping and little flashing blue light.
Signifying that we've been mentioned in a comment,
When it wakes you in the middle of the night.

I'm not saying its an easy habit to kick,
But there's a way to ease the addiction.
Occasionally, simply switch off your information device.
Life *will* feel better. And that's my prediction.

* * *

MY DAY OFF

It's Wednesday; it's 7 am; I'm going to get up early.
Twenty-four hours off work, and it's a glorious day.
Perhaps I'll finally clean the living room windows,
Which I've been putting off since the end of May.

Yes, I'm determined to get a few jobs finished,
Before everyone else wakes up and I'm interrupted.
For its better to complete what I need to get done,
Without being distracted and terminally disrupted.

The garden fence needs propping up at one end,
And a shelf in the bookcase is wobbling loose.
And what will I do with those two dozen Jaffas,
Which I promised to make freshly squeezed orange juice?

An hour has passed, and I'm still in bed,
Wondering if the windows can wait another week.
There are still some other things to get on with,
Like fixing the bath tap, which has developed a leak.

Just ten more minutes and I'll get out of bed,
I've still got plenty of time to get things done.
But I'm comfortable here with the bedroom window open,
Enjoying a gentle breeze and the warmth of the sun.

I'll stick the cushion covers in the washing machine,
That's at least one job I can cross off the list.
I mean, I really have to tend to one of my tasks,
Even if the more important ones have to be dismissed.

Another hour has gone, and I've missed breakfast,
And the idea of brunch is fast becoming a non-starter.
What began as an idea of a full and rewarding morning,
Has fast become a blueprint for a malingerer's charter.

It's definitely time to get up, get washed and dressed,
Before yet another day off disappears.
I shan't chastise myself for too much for my malaise,
As there's always the weekend to face my DIY fears.

* * *

SELF-INFLICTED SID

I can't begin to count the times I've self-inflicted pain,
By being unaware of my surroundings, not taking care.
It seems that if something can happen, it will happen,
My everyday life can leave me in total despair.

I'm sure we can all testify to the terrible, searing pain,
Of standing on a piece of Lego or 3-pin plug.
Well, I've done the pair in one manoeuvre,
And boy, it makes me feel like a total mug!

Like stubbing a toe on the bedroom door,
You know the pain is coming before you feel it.
It has a long way to travel, from the foot up to the brain,
Arggghhh! Then it hits, and your face can't conceal it.

Another thing I do quite a lot is accidentally bite my tongue,
Ever since a tough piece of steak pulled out a crown.
I can't even admit these cases are exclusive to eating,
Even when talking, teeth on the tongue clampdown.

Next on the list of injuries I bring on myself,
Has to be the paper cut, the scourge of digits and lips.
I only have to look at an unused envelope or take away menu,
And I get cold sweats from my head to my fingertips.

And then almost giving myself a heart attack,
When taking a trip to the loo, late at night.
With bleary eyes and brain still fast asleep,
I catch my reflection in the mirror and get quite a fright!

I've pulled muscles and sprained my wrists,
In the simple act of getting out of bed.
And the number of times I've tripped on a stair,
Or left a kitchen cupboard open and banged my head...

From stripping my tongue red raw after a packet of fizzy, sour sweets,
Burning my mouth on chillies and choking on peanuts,
To poking myself in the eye when I think I'm wearing glasses,
Home is a dangerous place when you're a total clutz.

* * *

PLANE ANNOYING

Don't sit next to me!! Don't sit next to me!!
Damn, that's all I need on a ten-hour flight.
An angry-looking boy plants himself down next to me,
Crying and arguing with eyes full of fight.

His mother tries in vain to calm the lad down,
His father looks like he's already given up the ghost.
Two weeks of hell, they have to look forward to,
Before we even cross over England's west coast.

However, the boy's behaviour is not my problem,
In eight hours, when we land in The States.
But it's hard to look beyond the here and now,
Trying not to imagine the horror that awaits.

A couple of elbows and a few kicks have made contact,
With several unguarded parts of my person.
We've just about cleared the Irish Sea,
And I just know it's only going to worsen.

An announcement is made, and lunch is served,
Perhaps it's time for some respite and peace.
No, he's complaining that he doesn't want to eat.
My levels of tolerance are beginning to decrease.

I give him a hard stare which confuses him for a moment.
He's in no doubt that I'm not one to be messed about.
But that bewildering moment is very brief and fleeting,
He kicks off again, ending his misbehaviour drought.

Looking over his head, I catch his mother's eye,
She mouths 'sorry' like that's going to appease.
'Try and control your annoying little brat',
I think, but don't say, continuing my increasing unease.

Later, a glorious hour of stillness ends abruptly,
With him awakening from a brief sleep with a start.
Curse the flight crew and their beverage service,
And their clattering, clunking service cart.

We're finally flying over the Canadian islands,
And I'm about to completely lose my cool.
One more kick or flailing elbow in my direction,
And I'm going to take this kid back to school.

The mother has gone off for a toilet break,
The father is at the end of the row, fast asleep.
So I surreptitiously nudge the kid's cup of coke over,
Which drenches his trousers, causing him to weep.

His father wakes up, and he's not best pleased,
And takes the little brat away to get cleaned up.
At last, a hiatus from the moaning and fidgeting,
I was beginning to think they'd be no letup.

On their return, they thankfully change around,
And the father kindly takes the boy's seat,
But the man develops a non-stop sneezing fit-
My abject misery is now totally complete.

* * *

TRANSFER DEADLINE DEBACLE

For six weeks, a football club has to sign a player,
Six whole weeks of the summer transfer window they've got.
So, why does it come down to the last twelve hours,
To figure out if they need that new striker or not?

As press and social media speculation heats up,
So, movement in the transfer market cools down.
The hope that your club will sign a top-class player,
Is dashed when they loan in a journeyman clown.

And, oh, the fuss that Sky Sports News makes,
As the clock counts down to the transfer deadline.
When the on/off deal of a reserve centre-back,
From Brighton to Southampton is the top headline.

The summer transfer window is a farce,
Most deals could be done in a week or two.
Better still, reduce the open window to a chink in the curtain,
A long weekend to get all their deals done will do.

* * *

CLICKBAIT-MANIA

Sometimes in life, 'you won't believe,
What doctors took out of a college student's ear'.
I saw a link instructing me to click on the link,
So, I felt it was my duty to press and adhere.

The page took almost 20 seconds to load,
And then I had to accept a multitude of cookies.
I'm then assaulted by dozens of ads,
For betting companies and high street bookies.

Page after page, click after click,
I search for a photo of this American lad.
What kind of horror has been plucked from his head?
What has befallen this poor undergrad?

Before I found the photo I'd been searching for,
For what seemed like a quarter of an hour,
I succumbed to the bombardment of advertisements,
And opened an account with Paddy Power.

At last, the article I'd been itching to see,
I started to feel like an ambulance chaser.
The underwhelming, disappointing foreign object-
Part of a pink pencil-top eraser.

Was that really it? What a waste of time,
I was totally hooked by clickbait; so brazen.
All to get me to sign up to a bookmaker,
Still, I won £30 on the 4.20 from Market Rasen.

* * *

BUCKING THE TREND

I don't know what people have got against me,
Is it because I don't tow the party line?
And won't conform to preconceived ideas,
I reckon it's because I've got a spine.

So, I prefer beef at Christmas and chicken at Easter,
That's no reason for people to get on my back.
And I make waffles on Shrove Tuesday. Big deal.
Besides,many folks ignore it and just make Jack.

If I'm out with friends at an Indian restaurant,
I'll order an omelette, as I don't like spicy food.
Unfortunately, it simply doesn't agree with me,
So, it's not because I'm difficult or being rude.

There are so many days dedicated to one thing or another,
It's hard to keep track of them, I admit.
So I carry on and plough my lone furrow,
And commemorate the day as I see fit.

On the first day of summer, I'll plan my winter holiday.
On St Patrick's Day, I'll crack open a bottle of Scotch.
On National No Smoking Day, I'll buy a packet of cigars
And smoke them on World Book Day in front of the TV I watch.

On the first day of the school Christmas holidays,
I take my kids out to buy new uniforms at first light.
At Halloween, when I open my door to trick or treaters,
It is them who I make sure get a good fright.

On all Saints Day, I'll listen to the Spice Girls,
That's one for the nineties' youth.
And I was so disappointed with the candidates in the local elections,
I blunted all the pencils in the voting booth.

Why should I do what society expects of me?
There's a dozen of these days they could drop.
That reminds me, today is National Poetry Day,
So, this seems like an ideal time to stop.

* * *

QUIZ NIGHT

The team meet up for another night of quizzing
At the local pub, our regular and favoured haunt.
'It looks to be a good turnout tonight,' says Gyp.
'I like a challenge. So bring it on!' he growls as a taunt.

We're still one short as the start time looms.
Joe is running late as he normally does.
'He'd better get here soon,' warms a concerned Sue.
Over the general hubbub, a perceptible buzz.

'I'm here, my people,' the missing Joe exclaims.
With arms wide open, an entrance he loves to make.
'Hurry and sit down; we're about to begin,' I say.
'I'll just get a drink,' His thirst he needs to slake.

Round one has finished, and we're tying for the lead.
Who knew the collective noun for bears is a sleuth?
And the translation for the Japanese parliament is "a diet",
We can't even put the blame on our misspent youth.

The film round is over, and we've picked up full points,
Things are looking good for a victory this week.
However, a nightmare set of questions on acronyms,
Drops us into third-for us, a position that is unique.

A break in proceedings is very much needed,
To rest and reset our collective quiz brain.
Matt disappears to the toilet; Joe nips to the bar,
Another round of drinks he goes to obtain.

Jimbo and I discuss our tactics at length,
We were struggling to get many answers right.
Perhaps our rampant cockiness is causing us to slip,
But we certainly won't give in without a fight.

Rounds on television and historical figures,
Put us well back on track for first prize.
Despite Joe's return to the bar and Matt's to the loo,
And Sue's decision to refill our snack supplies.

Mobile phones are out under the tables,
Of some teams who just can't keep pace.
Why do they even bother to take part in a quiz-
Only to cheat and still lose without grace?

Just one round to go, and happily, it's on sport,
Our nearest rivals don't look at all pleased.
We achieved full marks on my favourite subject,
And beyond the previous week's score, we eased.

Within ten minutes, we are declared the winners,
And a huge cheer goes up from the team.
Our prize—a meal for four in the pub carvery,
Ideal if getting meat sweats is your dream.

So another successful quiz night is over,
And another decisive victory is ours.
"Until next week then? "Jimbo rhetorically asks.
Is there any end to our supreme quizzing powers?

* * *

IT'S E.L.L.I.O.T!

It has Two Ls and just one T,
My name's on top of the page.
Why do you keep spelling it wrong?
Surely it's not that hard to engage.

Its common courtesy to spell a name right,
Especially as it's in front of your eyes.
Take a little time to learn all six letters,
And spell it right; give me a surprise.

If you hadn't been told, I would understand,
I suppose it's a simple mistake to make,
But when you've been shown the error of your ways,
It should be an elementary fault to shake.

So keep in mind those half dozen letters,
And the order in which they are arranged.
It's not Eliott, Elliott or Eliot, but ELLIOT,
To get that wrong now, you must be deranged.

* * *

THE EARLY BIRD CATCHES THE PLANE

'Our flight's not there,' I complained to my wife,
I looked up at the board, squinting my eyes.
'That's because it doesn't take off for almost six hours,'
She said in a way, fully intending to chastise.

'It's better to be early than to be late,' I said,
Attempting to justify my over-zealous time-keeping.
'It appeared that we're not the only ones,' she sighed,
Pointing at a group of youngsters on the floor, sleeping.

The terminal was quiet, as it should be at 5 am.
A dull whir of a floor polisher could be heard in the distance.
Suddenly a voice from behind caused us both to jump-
A uniformed lady asked, 'Can I be of assistance?'

'No, that's alright. Nice of you to ask,' I said.
'We're just a little bit early for our flight.'
'You can say that again,' my wife chipped in.
'Why do I feel like it's still 'last night'?'

'OK', I conceded. 'Perhaps I was a tad cautious.'
'You were.' The lady disappeared out of view.
'And *you* can stand here like a lemon,' said my wife.
'But I need a strong cup of coffee... or two.'

We walked to the coffee shop with luggage in tow,
Not passing another single passenger on the way.
Sat at a table in a deserted café, I perused the menu,
My wife ordered an espresso without delay.

We watched the concourse as the terminal began to fill,
With holidaymakers, retail workers and airport staff.
And a poor miserable couple trailing four young children,
All of them were arguing and shouting; I had to laugh.

Check-in was performed at the earliest possible time,
We almost got an upgrade due to a computer glitch.
Through passport control and security, we then passed,
Although a beeping X-ray machine caused me to twitch.

'Just over three hours to wait, eh?' my wife sighed,
As we started our saunter through Duty-Free.
'Oh look, a two-foot-long bar of Toblerone,' I exalted.
'Go crazy. Why don't you buy yourself two or three?'

I knew when the sarcasm started; I needed to back off,
And I've learnt over the years to stay quiet.
It *was* my decision to arrive at the airport so early,
And the last thing I wanted was to cause a one-on-one riot.

After a couple of hours of frosty malevolence,
A warm front began heading my way.
'This time tomorrow, I'll be sitting by the pool,' she said.
The fact that the forecast was for rain, I decided not to say.

At last, the call to the boarding gate went out,
Naturally, it was the one furthest from where we were.
I set out with my duty-free and reasonably happy wife,
The wrath of whom I'd been careful not to incur.

We arrived at gate 57, and we took a well-earned rest,
Along with the other passengers waiting to board.
Amongst them was the miserable couple from earlier on,
Their kids at least were now quiet; thank the Lord!

Boarding began, and we joined the queue,
My wife laughed, 'You know you've left something behind?'
Something was missing from my duty-free bags-
My massive Toblerone! Her comment was most unkind.

Once on the plane, I buckled myself in,
And watched the other passengers find their places.
The inclement weather made a grim view from the window,
As did the looks on the miserable couple's faces.

Once everyone was seated, the first officer announced,
Take-off was delayed due to the weather getting worse.
'This is all your fault,' my wife unfairly uttered.
I said nothing, beginning to think I must be under a curse.

Half an hour went by, and we were still at the gate,
We hadn't taxied; we hadn't even moved an inch.
My wife confirmed, 'You're to blame for this, you know?'
In a low inflexion that caused me to tense up and flinch.

I said, 'The next time we fly, we'll stay at an on-site hotel,
So we won't have to worry about being late.'
'I wasn't worried. It was *you* who was panicking.
And it's *your* fault I'm in this state.'

'I'm afraid to announce that due to this bad weather...'
The first officer spoke over the PA again.
'The flight has been delayed. We're terribly sorry.'
We then had to get up and disembark the plane.

'You can't blame me for that,' I told my angry wife,
As we trudged our way back to the terminal building.
There was no point in me trying to lighten her mood,
And it was impossible to find a lily that needed gilding.

'There's one silver lining, a positive point,'
I exclaimed in a triumphant, nay celebratory tone.
At least I can go back to the duty-free shop now,
And buy me another two-foot-long Toblerone!

* * *

I ONLY WANTED A KORMA

'I'll have my usual, please,' I told the waiter.
He wrote down, "One chicken korma."
'You should try something else, nothing too hot,
Just something a little bit warmer.'

'But I like my korma. I always have,'
I told him, catching his eye.
'Maybe a passanda or a bhuna; they're nice.
Or a tasty lamb korai?'

'Maybe next time,' I lied to him.
He was becoming a little bit haughty.
'Rogan Josh, a keema with peas, you'll like.
Or perhaps, a vegetable balti?'

'I want chicken korma, plain and simple.
Surely, you get my thread?'
The waiter just smiled, thought for a moment-
'A biryani and a keema naan bread?'

'I know what you'd like,' he continued
"You can't say no to the Dhansak, sir.'
'Oh, I bloody well could," I sneered in return,
'I think I told you what I'd prefer.'

'Right. You win; I won't have a korma.'
The waiter just nodded his head.
'But I don't want a balti or anything else.
I'm off to the Chinese instead.'

* * *

WAKE UP! IT'S THREE IN THE MORNING

With alarming regularity over the last year or so,
After three hours, I'll wake up from my sleep.
And there's nowt I can do to return to my slumber,
Not deep breathing, meditation or counting sheep.

I can retire at 10 pm or two in the morning,
The outcome is the same every night.
A dream comes to an end, and I open my eyes,
The same scenario I endure without respite.

Usually, by this time, my wife has long gone,
Fed up with me fidgeting and snoring.
In the spare room next door, she'll resume her kip,
Lowering her desire to hit me from soaring.

Could it be insomnia? No, I ruled that one out,
As I normally doze off without much trouble.
It's my body clock's snooze alarm I can't turn off,
My efforts to find the button will have to redouble.

Apart from keeping a tally of those ovine beasts,
Other methods I have tried to no avail.
Including banging my head 20 times on a pillow,
Something I was told would be guaranteed not to fail.

Of course, there are sleeping pills and herbal tablets,
Warm milky drinks and lavender oil,
But getting to the land of nod isn't the problem.
It's the inability to stay there that makes my blood boil.

But, there is a plus point, one positive note,
Of waking up during the night.
For if I hadn't this problem and slept right through,
There would not be a poem to write.

* * *

THE LAST LOST LIST

'Not again? It's the third time you've done that.'
My wife complained as I handed over the shopping.
'I'm afraid I forgot the list again, so I improvised.'
I expected she'd get a bit mad, but I hoped, not hopping.

I thought I pretty much knew what she wanted.
Because I picked up the list to take a cursory glance.
Before putting it down and leaving it on the sideboard,
So it's not like I completely played a game of chance.

She started unpacking the many plastic bags,
Someone was not happy; about that I quickly knew.
Because she expelled several deep and audible sighs,
"What *is* the point of making a list for you?"

I had no doubt she needed potatoes,
But the ones I bought were "baking", not "new".
As she saw the button mushrooms instead of Portobello,
She grumbled, 'You know, you haven't got a clue.'

39

'I remembered the lettuce' I chipped in, looking for points.
'That's an Iceberg when I wanted Romaine.'
'Ah well, I picked up your bottle of bubbly,' I countered.
'You bought cheap Cava when I requested Champagne.'

I remembered the trifle, albeit raspberry, not strawberry.
I remembered the flour, albeit self-raising, not plain.
I remembered the soup, although it was vegetable, not tomato.
I remembered the rice, although it was Basmati, not long grain.

'At least I think I got the milk order right,' I said.
'Almost. There *was* the word "skimmed" on my list.
She held up and showed me the blue-topped bottle.
'But I wanted *semi*-skimmed. The prefix, you missed.'

The next few items out of the bags, I got spot on,
And her mood was visibly getting lighter.
Until she picked out the selection of *economy* fruit yoghurts,
'Dear, oh dear.You're definitely getting tighter.'

'The oil is extra virgin olive. I wanted sunflower.
The bread is medium. I wanted thick cut.
I didn't ask for jam. I wanted marmalade.
But, at least you remembered my Fruit & Nut.'

'What is this?" she spat, holding up a pre-wrapped bird.
"If I'm not very much mistaken, it's a chicken.'
'I wrote down 'eight boneless chicken thighs', you fool.'
The wife's full temper was about to kick in.'

'I bought the fabric conditioner you like, see.'
'Right brand, wrong fragrance for my clothes.
I like the one with the summer breeze aroma,
Not this one with that reeks of alpine meadows.'

I gulped and stood back another couple of feet,
The last bag– and I saw what was peaking through.
'What's this? A child's birthday celebration cake?'
I must admit, *that* was a surprise to me too.

'Had you remembered my list, this would not have happened.
Half the items you forgot. Most of the others weren't right.
And what's this? I wanted half a dozen fresh, round rolls,
Not hamburger baps- and they're wholemeal, not even white.'

'I'll tell you what', I said, 'next time, *you* do the weekly shop.
That might prevent your incessant, terrible mood.'
'You've got a point,' she said. 'I think I'll do that.'
'But you'll be living in your car and foraging for your own food.'

* * *

YOU COULDN'T WRITE THE SCRIPT

'You couldn't write the script.'
Without a doubt, my cliché du jour.
Sports commentators love to quote,
As their excited voices soar.

Like 'You couldn't make it up.'
That is precisely what you must do,
To extol the excitement, you convey,
By making a sweeping statement true.

Because if every situation was the same,
Then no script would need to be penned.
Things would play out as per usual,
And no drama would have the right to ascend.

To sum up and to conclude my assertion,
And to make matters abundantly clear-
A script certainly needs to be written,
If toward "out of the ordinary" you wish to steer.

* * *

WANNA PLAY CHICKEN?

I'm driving home at night; a vehicle is approaching me head-on.
Who's going to give way? The conclusion is far from foregone.

He's not stopping. Well, I'm not going to give way.
It's not my job to keep his road rage at bay.

He's less than 100 metres away. So who is gonna blink first?
I'm not usually this confrontational. Mildly antagonistic at worst.

But I'm almost home. Just a left at the end of the road,
I don't care where he's going, but this is my postcode.

I'm sure there's not enough width for two vehicles to compete,
Not with parked cars on both sides of a residential street.

He's coming right at me; I might have to let him pass,
Unless our distance judgment is unbelievably world-class.

Suddenly he slows down and flashes me with his headlights
Then pulls into the kerb just as I was about to give him his last rites.

I drive past whilst giving him the driver's wave
To make him aware that I know how to behave.

Damn! I should have flashed. It's far too dark to see me.
Now he'll think I'm rude. I should make an apology.

But it's too late now; I can see his tail lights in my mirror,
I could have given him a couple of toots if he's been nearer.

I feel a bit guilty now, and he probably regrets his decision,
To give this inconsiderate oaf the right of way to avoid a collision.

It could be the final straw; he's lost faith in all humanity,
And the air inside of his car is filled with every conceivable profanity.

Perhaps I'm over-reacting, and he hasn't paid any attention,
To my apparent non-affirmation of his generous intervention.

Although, it wouldn't surprise me if next time, he'll think twice
Than to yield to another vehicle, well, my car, to be precise.

So, if a similar situation arises, I'll make sure I'll flash,
To let the oncoming car pass without a possibility of a crash.

Because a little thoughtful gesture goes an awful long way.
To keep that nasty spectre of road rage at bay.

* * *

INCLEMENCY REIGNS

From the gentle pitter-patter of raindrops,
To the crashing majesty of a raging storm,
There's something incredibly satisfying for me-
In a country where bad weather seems the norm.

The watery glow of autumn sunrise,
It is, of course, a sight to behold and admire.
Or to feel the heat of the sun on pale, cool skin,
After months of dark, cold days, we all aspire.

But the sheer drama of what nature has to offer,
Thrills me more than calm, warm placidity.
A bolt of lightning, a booming explosion of thunder,
Excites me, immediately banishing all torpidity.

Sitting in a car when a swirling wind whips up,
And the vehicle shaking from side to side,
Strangely brings me certain peace and calm,
A serenity a blue-skied day can't provide.

It may sound a little bit childish,
But I still count the seconds in my head.
Between the sudden blinding flash of lightning,
And the crash of thunder that many dread.

Sleet, hail and snow can be just as wondrous,
As the beautiful sunny days that we all savour.
And while I don't decry those who prefer the latter,
I'm an advocate of weather of a slightly more sinister flavour.

* * *

POSITIVELY DOUBTFUL

I KNOW my sharp mind is in a haze.
My glass is DEFINITELY half full *or* half empty.
I'll UNQUESTIONABLY do what needs to be done if I have no other
option.
I am POSITIVE that I haven't decided.
I am SURE that I have no opinion.
I have NO doubt there might be concerns.
My PRECISE description may be a little vague.
I am RESOLUTE that I have questions
Let me make it ABSOLUTELY CLEAR that I'm unsure.
I am CONFIDENT in my diffidence.
I am OPTIMISTIC in my pessimism.
But, I UNEQUIVOCALLY believe my mind might change.
So, in closing and just to confirm to all-
I'm CONVINCED that I'm 100% UNDENIABLY, INDUBITABLY
EXPRESSLY, EXPLICITLY uncertain of my actions.

* * *

ASK A SILLY QUESTION

How long is a piece of string?
It's two-foot six. Please prove me wrong.

How long is a piece of string??
It's twice as long as half its length.

How long is a piece of string???
It's as long as you want it to be.

OK then, how long is my tether?
I don't know, but I feel you're coming to the end of it.

* * *

TEN COMMANDMENTS OF THE ENGLAND FAN

To be a true 'fan' nowadays, there are certain rules to adhere.
To support England and show your allegiance to the flag.
And these ten commandments must be followed during a tournament.
You don't have to be a real football fan, not in the traditional sense,
But these commandments will see you well and prove you truly believe.

The First Commandment
Thou must be ever-present on social media and change your profile pic.
A cross of St George, or maybe Harry Kane or Bobby Moore in a triumphant pose are acceptable.

The Second Commandment
Thou must declare 'It's coming home!' wherever and whenever.
Three words. Three simple words, but three strong, defiant and meaningful words.

The Third Commandment
Thou must complain about being at work and missing the game, even if you secretly find that watching Love Island is preferable to watching a game.

The Fourth Commandment
Thou must paint the faces of your young and then oneself. Not too well, of course; the application should be able to flake off within 10 minutes.

The Fifth Commandment
Thou must order a pizza ten minutes before half-time of the match and thou must jump up and down like an angry meerkat when it takes an hour to arrive.

Commandments six to 10 apply to pub gardens and fan parks, where all inhibitions are banished
Beware -This is where the occasional followers collide with the seasoned, hardcore fans.

The Sixth Commandment
Thou must lose control and toss beer and cups into the air whenever our brave boys score a goal, without even waiting for a V.A.R decision.

The Seventh Commandment
Tables must be climbed and jumped upon as soon as the beer deluge has reduced to a mere amber drizzle.

The Eighth Commandment

When England score a goal, (and they will) - shirts and tops must be removed by all males.
They must then be waved around in a circular motion, like a football rattle in days of yore.

The Ninth Commandment

The Patriot's Commandment. Thou must spontaneously break into singing the National Anthem, and be off-key with your arms stretched out, eyes fixed to the heavens.

The Tenth Commandment

The most important commandment of all. The rule no England fan can ignore.
When any group is gathered in any garden, fan park or stadium, thou must all sing 'Three Lions' in unison –
Whereas as the first commandment instructs us to merely repeat the promise,
Number ten requires us to sing it- loudly, proudly and patriotically. It's our duty as England fans.
However, only the chorus, as not to upset the swathes of part-time fans who do not know the rest of the song.

Moses bought down the Ten Commandments from Mount Sinai on two tablets of stone.
But the origins of the Ten Commandments of English football fandom are shrouded in mystery.
They are not written or inscribed; they are not produced in any visible form.

However, heed them, act on them for as long as England remain in a tournament.

Only when they are knocked out will you be allowed to ignore football again and return to Love Island.

* * *

THE BIG WIMBLEDON QUESTION

I take a keen interest in the Wimbledon Championships.
The tour's top event I love to watch.
From the opening rounds to the final Sunday,
The quality of tennis is top-notch.

But there's a question that has always bugged me,
For a good forty years, I'd say,
It's not why they waited so long to roof centre court,
Or why they don't play on the middle Sunday.

Its what happens to all the bottles,
Of Robinson's Barley water that sit there,
Being ignored by all and sundry,
On the back of the umpire's chair.

Has any player, official, ball boy or girl,
Ever made up a cup to drink?
Or is it, at the end of a hot day's play,
Just simply poured down the sink?

A cup of orange or lemon barley water.
Is quite refreshing to drink on a hot day.
But just imagine a player requesting a cup,
The poor ballboy or girl wouldn't know what to do or say.

The sight of those bottles of Robinson's,
Standing proud through downpours and drought,
Provoke me to wonder year after year,
If any of it will ever be poured out.

* * *

A LATE WAIT

I have always tried my best to never be late,
For a meeting, an appointment, a date or a mate.
Being on time shows a certain respect,
And an image of reliability you want to reflect.

The world is full of people sitting and waiting,
For meetings, lunches, or even dating.
Staring at watches and the time on their phone,
Expecting a text to reschedule or postpone.

Sitting alone in a restaurant isn't a joy,
And waiting for a guest does certainly annoy,
The party who managed to get there when agreed.
Perhaps good timekeepers are a dying breed.

'Your courier delivery will arrive this morning'.
Is the email you'll get as a way of warning.
To expect your package by the latest, midday,
By mid-afternoon - a third emailed apology for the delay.

It's not only people who don't care if they're late,
Refunds and repayments also infuriate.
If you owe a bank money, they'll take it right away,
But it's five working days if it's them who has to pay.

I guess it's just the way the world is going,
People will wait to see from where the wind is blowing.
Before deciding to get somewhere on time.
After all, where does it say that tardiness is a crime?

Call me old-fashioned, but I still like to be,
On time for a dinner or afternoon tea.
But maybe its too much to ask others to take heed,
It's just good manners to show up when agreed.

* * *

EXCORCISING THE GARAGE

I stepped into the abyss; the day had arrived,
It was time to release the garage from its bondage of crap.
I pulled up the door and stood aghast in disbelief.
I'll need to watch my step in this dastardly death trap.

Do I really want to keep anything, or can it all go?
It was tough to spy anything that I still needed.
Certainly not the old 26-inch TV or ancient light fittings,
And I'll never again use the busted Walkman, I conceded.

A rarely used zed bed, an electric heater without a plug,
And an incomplete collection of earthenware plates,
Placed on top of a plastic box of old toddler's clothes,
Leaning on a couple of rusting baby safety gates.

A shopping bag containing my Grandma's kitchen utensils,
In a plastic crate that once transported beers.
I don't think she'll ever want them back again,
After all, she's been dead for nearly twenty-five years.

Little football figures, I collected for fun,
A cheap, white desk fan with a splintered base,
A selection of photo frames, once given as a gift,
And a chrome-edged wall clock with a wonky, warped face.

Why did I think these items would be useful one day?
Did I imagine they'd regain a place back in my home?
And as for the DVD player with the snapped off drawer-
Just as useful as the two-foot-high, headless gnome.

In front of the garage, parked on the driveway,
Sits a small, yellow skip, just waiting for junk.
But where do I start and what goes in first-
The old kitchen sink or porcelain elephant sans its trunk?

An hour into the task, and little space is being created.
I want the memory of a cluttered garage to be erased.
But as one piece of rubbish is thrown in the skip,
I turn around, and it's been miraculously replaced.

Rain damaged books and old birthday cards,
The kid's old board games neatly stacked.
Why are they there? I have no idea.
None of them are complete, with all pieces intact.

A bicycle, a tricycle with one wheel between them,
Hang rusting and unloved on the rear wall.
They were the next redundant items to be dispatched,
After almost tripping over a punctured leather football.

Newspapers from the day my kids were born,
Empty toilet rolls and a box of crushed candles.
Boxless tapes of the cassette and VHS kind,
And a couple of saucepans without handles.

An empty pencil case, a small, crushed lampshade,
A tall wooden speaker with a blown amp.
An oil can, two pairs of glasses, both without lenses,
And a black sack of clothes left in the damp.

A child's Winnie-the-Pooh sit-on train,
With the still functioning but muffled hooter.
And in the corner, upside-down and severely dented -
The housing from my first home computer.

There must be something worth keeping,
In this dire antithesis of an Aladdin's Cave.
The football magazines from the 80s perhaps,
Or what is left of the old living room architrave?

No, they've all got to go; I must be ruthless,
And get this garage back to its original state.
A clear space in which to park my car,
And it won't be too long, at this rate.

Two hours later and the task is complete,
And I've just finished sweeping the floor.
The skip's full to the brim of miscellaneous rubbish,
I think I'll now tackle the attic as an encore.

* * *

DENTIST

A visit to the dentist is something many fear.
But I don't mind if it's just twice a year.

It's not the drilling or discomfort I most hate,
But the effect on my wallet I nervously await.

When the man with the drill buzzing in his hand.
Says "you need some work," then it ain't so grand.

Two fillings have fallen out, and a crown has, aswell.
And there's a bit of root canal– There's the bombshell!

'Are you feeling any distress? Is anything causing you pain?'
No, but my bank account might when funds begin to drain.

'Let's do a couple of X-rays'. That'll bump up the bill.
'Perhaps an appointment with the hygienist.' He's going in for the kill.

After an hour in the chair and another one to come,
I thank the dentist although my mouth is still numb,

To the receptionist, I shuffle with debit card in hand.
How much abuse can my bank account withstand?

'Until next time,' I mumble as she hands my card back.
My poor current account, just barely in the black.

She smiles as I leave the surgery and out into the sun.
The damage to my finances has only just begun.

* * *

I CAN'T BELIEVE...

I can't believe it's been a week...
Since we bought our two babies home.
Look at them - they're so tiny and sweet,
As they sleep so silently, unable to roam.

I can't believe it's been a year...
Their first birthday has come around so fast.
Look at them - so happy and carefree,
Sitting up in their high chairs, at last.

I can't believe they're three years old...
They grow bigger day by day.
Look at them playing in harmony,
The terrible twos -Ha, what are they?

I can't believe they're five years old...
The terrible twos came around a little late.
Look at them shoving and poking each other,
And stealing food from each other's plate.

I can't believe they're eight years old...
They bicker and evoke one another's wrath.
Look at them argue about who's sitting where
And whose turn it is next, for the bath.

I can't believe they're ten years old...
They're in to double figures, at last.
Look at our girl straightening her brother's school tie
From two years ago, it's such a pleasant contrast.

I can't believe they're 11 years old...
And take a bus on to secondary school.
Look at our girl dropping our boy's school tie
Into a puddle; she's fed up with him playing the fool.

I can't believe they're 14 years old...
They might be leaving school in a couple of years.
Look at our boy hiding his sister's homework.
I can guarantee it's going to end up in tears.

I can't believe they're 15 years old...
They'll be taking their GCSEs before we know.
Look at our daughter help her brother with his homework.
I'm sure he appreciates all she does, though.

I can't believe they're 16 years old...
Their final days at school are nigh.
Loving siblings and best friends now,
How quickly sixteen years has flown by.

* * *

CASINO

The sights, the lights and even the frights,
From young adulthood, I've come to adore.
For me, nothing at all can possibly replicate,
The excitement of the casino floor.

As much as I love the electricity and pomp,
Of an occasional fun night on the spiel,
There are plenty of deluded souls around the joint,
Hoping for a life-changing spin of a roulette wheel.

The incessant songs of the slot machines,
Meld together to make a musical jumble.
As patrons desperately continue their task,
For more cash, in their wallets they'd fumble.

Sitting serenely in seats that vibrate and rock,
In front of virtual wheels that spin and freeze.
Buffalos, tigers, exotic birds and dragons,
The menagerie of symbols relentlessly tease.

Some players are happy enough to win their stake back,
And they'll stand up and leave without distress.
While others will doggedly feed the machine,
With just how much dough is anyone's guess.

Others like to try their hand at the blackjack table,
Feeling they have more than a reasonable chance,
Of being dealt a hand to beat the dealer,
Although they're often lead a merry dance.

A King and a Queen −the player delights!
That'll surely be enough to win the hand.
But after a 10, the dealer flips an ace,
The punter's joy is immediately canned.

At least when playing on the blackjack table,
You can bet at a leisurely pace.
Win a bit here, lose a bit there,
With nobody getting in your face.

That kind of serenity is rarely afforded,
Around the roulette table, where people are sprawled.
Stacks of coloured chips strewn across the baize.
In desperation, before 'no more bets' is called.

'Colour!' bawls an impatient player,
And he throws a wad of notes down on the table.
The croupier slides him five towers of chips,
And he covers as many numbers as he's able.

In no time at all, his handsome cityscape,
Has reduced to the size of a bungalow.
As good fortune has decided to pass him by.
The language of desperate punter starts to flow.

'How can "red" come up five times in a row?
The next spin *has* to be black.'
Is the futile muttering of the desperate punter,
Whose very spirit is about to crack.

Of course, there are other games to try,
Like craps, baccarat and pai gow.
But I haven't a clue on how they are played,
They're far too complicated and highbrow.

I'll just walk down the banks of amazing slots,
And choose one with the most interesting creatures.
And I'll take out a "twenty" and feed the machine,
In the hope of scoring those bonus features.

It's a knack to know when to quit,
And to cease adding to the casino's wealth.
Because betting the last of your earnings,
Really isn't good for your financial health.

* * *

LOST

Keys, wallets, phones and glasses; I've lost the lot.
Some say it's been a while since I completely lost the plot.
'Where's the last place you saw it?' folk would try to assist.
If I knew that, then it'd no longer be lost. Wow! There's a twist.

I've lost my phone when it's been in my hand.
I've lost the remote control when it's been on the TV stand.
I've lost my glasses when they've been on my head.
I've lost the ability to sleep when I've been lying in bed.

I've lost my debit card when it's in the chip and pin machine.
I've lost sweet and sour chicken in beef in black bean.
I've lost my petrol cap when it's on top of the car.
I've lost my pint of bitter when it's on top of the bar.

Whether I continue to lose things is not in doubt,
Like forgetting my password, just as I log out.
Most things I mislay are rarely actually lost,
It's just down to my frozen mind, which needs to defrost.

* * *

MY DRUNK BARBER

Cutting and snipping; pouring and sipping,
My drunk barber plies his trade.
Chatting and chirping; farting and burping,
The inebriated master of the blade.

Brushing and combing, coughing and foaming,
The barber makes a nasty mishap.
'Cause of beering whilst shearing; my pain began searing
As my left ear dropped into my lap.

* * *

RAIN MANAGEMENT

British football managers- you can always tell them,
They're the ones who don't shield from the rain.
When their foreign counterparts pull up a hood,
The act of keeping dry, the Brits treat with disdain.

I think it's something to do with a comradeship,
That they want to share with their players.
'If you're getting wet, then I will too.'
And wear the bare minimum of layers.

As the rain lashes down, in a shirt and jacket,
To the referee, the Brit manager will shout and bitch.
From the touchline as the rain pelts down heavier,
Getting soaked along with the guys on the pitch.

The foreign coaches wear heavy coats,
To keep the inclement weather at bay.
And in the cold winter will even zip them up,
Showing their British equivalents the way.

Those foreign bosses aren't such martyrs,
The Germans, the Italians and certainly the French,
They don't have the desire to get rained on-
And their designer suits, no need to drench.

Would our home-grown bosses look weak and distant,
Just for wearing a cap on their head?
And to keep their perfectly coiffured hair dry,
For the post-match interview that they dread.

* * *

PHONE SCAMMERS

The only ones who still call on my landline,
Are my mother and those who try to deceive.
It could be the "bank", the "council" or a "household survey",
But 'broken broadband' is the one I most usually receive.

Before one hears a voice, there is the curious silence,
For around 10 seconds before it becomes clear.
Then comes the deafening hubbub of a large office,
Provoking me to remove the phone from my ear.

'Hello, my name is John/Jack/Peter/Frank,'
Says an Asian voice sounding cold and bland.
'I'm calling from BT/Virgin/a made up company,
There's a problem with your household broadband.'

'Have I?' I'll reply, without a hint of sarcasm,
'But I'm not even with your company, you know?'
A short pause and a rustle of paper will follow,
He'll just ignore me and then continue his flow.

'Can you get to a computer, where you are?'
He'll ask me next, without exception.
'I'm in front of my laptop right now,' I'll lie,
Giving him the green light to continue his deception.

He'll pause for a moment, not believing his luck;
I mean, it's the least I can do– to waste his time.
Then he'll continue the ruse, in typical fashion,
In an attempt to fleece me through crime.

He'll ask me to type something into the search bar,
I'll wonder if he understands what he's asking.
But, I'll keep up the pretence; my little fish hooked,
Biding my time until my grand unmasking.

Oh, I love to have a bit of self-indulgent fun,
At the dastardly phone scammers expense.
I'll let him finish him well-rehearsed chat,
Before a few choice words, I'll gleefully dispense.

I might call him a moron or something equally tame,
Not that it would register in his addled brain.
But, when he's in full flow, reading off his script,
I'll chuck in something a little more profane.

I like to play the part of a complete idiot,
Not knowing the caps lock from delete.
And as I hear the scammer's frustration rise,
I'll squawk a brief animal noise as a treat.

"I don't think it's plugged in," I'll ruefully confess.
At this point, the scammer assumes he's been rumbled.
Then I'll be called all the choice names under the sun,
How I will laugh, knowing his attempt fraud has crumbled.

The line will go dead, and I'll put the phone down,
And wonder what he was trying to get out of me.
And who actually falls for such inane duplicity?
A question I might ask the next Bill, Steve or Lee.

* * *

EXCEPTIONALLY HIGH LEVELS OF BULLSHIT

No matter what company or organisation I call,
The recorded message is invariably the same.
It's announced in the most sympathetic tone, of course.
But I know it's all a part of their collective game.

'Due to the exceptionally high rate of calls, we're getting,
You may be waiting for longer than usual right now.'
That means, 'We haven't got the staff any more to talk to you.
Don't waste your time; just end your call. Ciao.'

But you'll get the same message whenever you call.
Believe me; I've tried at all hours of the day and night.
Even outside of office hours at three in the morning.
It's always the same, even though no one's there on site.

Whether it's an insurance company, the bank, or the local council,
The words may differ, but the message is clear-
'Thanks for calling, but please leave us alone.
I'm afraid nobody wants to speak to you here.'

* * *

POSTAL DELAY

The days of an early morning postal delivery,
Have disappeared into the mists of time.
To receive any letters any time before noon,
Nowadays, it would be something quite sublime.

A few years ago, in the early afternoon,
Postie would appear with his red bin of mail.
And a handful of assorted junk he'd deliver,
Including a daily pizza menu, without fail.

Not long after that, we wouldn't see the postman,
Before tea time on any given weekday.
With a pleasant disposition and a 'good afternoon.'
He'd hand you your mail and be merrily on his way.

But now he doesn't arrive until the evening,
Perhaps to coincide with the rush hour's hurly-burly.
I can't understand why our mail comes so late.
But then, actually, it could about 12 hours early.

* * *

THEY'VE STARTED... THEY'VE STOPPED

I woke one morning with eyes so bleary they could barely focus,
But it wasn't my vision that interrupted my slumber.
The sound of angle grinders and sledgehammers were the disturbers,
Along with workmen shouting, I was unaware of the number.

It took a good five minutes to build up the composure,
To throw off my snug duvet and get to my feet.
And with a squint and yawn, I peered out of the window,
To see what was happening on my usually quiet street.

At last! They're finally replacing the broken paving stones,
That have been cracking and splintering for a dozen years.
A stack of pristine white, oblong slabs await their turn,
The glorious din was now music to my ears.

I watched in wonderment as the workmen continued their task,
Of making the walkway outside my house, non-hazardous once again.
With broad Irish accents, their loud joyous chat adds to the cacophony,
But as long as they do a good job, I for one, won't complain.

After my breakfast and now through the living room window,
I watched them set out yellow plastic barriers and red warning signs.
The grass verge was being filled, and the kerb was taken up,
Four of them working hard; just one, standing on the sidelines.

An hour later, the jolly band had disappeared from the scene.
A clean, gum-less collection of paving is waiting to be christened.
Perhaps they'd be back after lunch, or maybe I won't see them again.
Oh, to that little negative voice in my head, I really should have
listened.

A lunch hour came and went, even allowing for a generous extension,
But no workmen returned to the open, borderless verge.
I imagined they might come back to following day to complete,
But no such luck, to finish their assignment, there was no urge.

So now, 23 lunch breaks later, the kerb is still missing,
And the yellow fencing still surrounds the incomplete jobs.
I wonder if I shall ever see or be awoken again by the gang,
And the boisterous row that came out of their collective gobs.

* * *

WASHING MACHINE

The washing machine, at last, is silent.
Peace and quiet have momentarily returned.
I can hear the birds in the garden now.
The constant whir of that white box adjourned.

But now the tumble drier joins in,
Although at a few decibels lower.
But right on cue, the loose zip rattles around,
Sounding like a golf ball chewed up in a mower.

The washer's been off for an hour now,
But another load is ready to go in.
Freshly bought down from the bathroom,
From the almost overflowing laundry bin.

A fully loaded machine is about to go.
The return to peace and quiet will take a while.
With a washing tablet and conditioner at the ready.
This is not a choice; this has become a lifestyle.

* * *

I DO LIKE MONDAYS

Tell me why, I don't like Mondays…
Well, I'll tell you why they're not all that bad.
They shouldn't be subject to our derision,
And the reason why we start the week so sad.

To begin with, many Mondays aren't spent at work,
Less than any other day, bar Sunday; it's true.
Take four of them out of your holiday allowance,
And they start to feel better for you.

Include Easter Monday and the two in May,
And reduce the unfounded feelings of fear.
Of the most condemned 24-hours of the week.
So, enjoy yourselves; crack open a beer!

If you're lucky and if the calendar dictates,
Christmas and New Year can fall just right.
Adding *another* couple of Mondays to the list,
Even though on the latter one, you might feel a bit shite.

And when you add August bank holiday into the equation,
You'll see that they don't deserve such hate.
Making a potential total of 10; a fifth of all Mondays,
-To give my argument a little extra weight.

Now, the real villain of the piece here is Tuesday,
The crappy lining of every dark cloud.
But, 'Tell me why, I don't like Tuesdays,'
Just doesn't sound right when sung out loud.

* * *

PLEASE DON'T BRING ME FLOWERS

Please don't bring me flowers,
For an anniversary or my birthday.
They're not something I want to have,
Not even if I'm ill or in a bad way.

Roses and posies and chrysanthemums too,
Might look nice in a vase on a shelf.
But they're not the things I want to see.
You're best off keeping them for yourself.

They completely play havoc with my sinuses.
And can make me cough and sneeze.
If I'm desperate for the aroma of flora,
I'll enjoy a few sprays of Febreze.

I hope I don't sound ungrateful and rude,
But I've simply never seen the point,
Of spending any amount of money on plant life,
Not even if it's dried and rolled-up in a joint.

Don't get me wrong; I appreciate the thought,
Of buying me anything of any description.
But if you feel the urge to buy me a gift,
How about a 12-month Netflix subscription?

Sorry, but I felt you should be told,
That any plant will die within hours,
And then it will end up with the garden waste,
So, my request to you -please don't bring me flowers.

* * *

OVER THE HILL AT 50

They used to say that life begins at 40,
Well, according to some companies, it's ending at 50.
Just look at the plethora of adverts that always appear on TV.

A raft of over 50s life insurance ads,
And funeral plans, there are tons.
If it's not *your* death they're after; it certainly *is* someone's.

The actors used in these commercials,
Are often good looking, shiny and fit,
Apart from the one for Sun Life, the senile, surprised old git.

His mail is always posted next door,
But June's on hand to bring it around,
To the simpering fool holding binoculars, she loves to astound.

These ads are usually shown during the day,
Do they think the retirement age has dropped,
To a mere half-century? It's a long time before their clogs are popped.

'Don't be a burden on your family',
These funeral plan ads want us to feel,
What a comforting thought that is, during a break in Dickinson's Real
Deal.

The free gift for simply applying once was a pen,
But now a £100 gift card can be yours.
Of course, if it's not delivered through your neighbours' front doors.

These ads come so thick and fast,
They leave me feeling I'm at great harm.
But at least I'm not ready for meals delivered by those folks at
Wiltshire Farm.

* * *

WHY ARE YOU SO SURPRISED?

We Brits seem to be constantly surprised,
By the most obvious things; questions aren't disguised.
'It's getting dark at four,' someone is bound to say.
As if deep winter has never before passed our way.

'It's amazing! It's been a year since your birthday,' is another great one.
If one waited and thought a moment, those words might just stun.
'The kids are growing up so fast; it's just unreal.'
Human children do that a lot; it's no big deal.

'Chocolate bars are getting smaller than they were in my youth.'
Perhaps your hands are getting bigger; that's nearer the truth.
'Oh my God, we lose an hour's sleep on Sunday morning'
It happens every spring. Watch the news; you'll get a warning.

'I can't believe that MPs get away with lying for so long.'
That's what politicians do. They don't know right from wrong.
'I see in The Budget that petrol and fags have gone up again.'
Like they have done every year since about 1910.

'England lose on penalties again. How unlucky are we?'
As if it was going to be easy and virtually carefree.
'Aren't policemen looking younger? They're barely out of school.'
The truth is that *you're* getting older, you silly old fool.

'Do you know it's six months until Christmas Day?'
Well, it's the 25th of June. So that's normally the way.
I guess it's part of being British to be surprised at regular events.
I could be exaggerating a bit, but I just wanted to add my two cents.

* * *

POST MATCH DRIVEL

I regularly make the same old complaint,
When a reporter asks a combatant after a game.
Are you happy with the win /did you deserve to lose?
What on earth do they expect them to claim?

The inane questions draw bland answers,
From footballers and managers who are at great pains,
To play down a victory or play up a defeat,
False modesty and defensiveness reigns.

And is there a genre of TV entertainment,
Where such cliched responses are so excepted?
From 'it was a game of two halves', and 'the boys did well',
To 'I got 101 per cent effort, that's all I expected.'

I long to hear a manager say one day,
When asked if he was unhappy with a loss.
After taking a deep breath, they'd honestly reply,
'Sure, I'm absolutely thrilled with that old dross.'

Banal interviews aren't exclusive to football,
But they're the ones I most regularly see.
If you've nothing worth saying, say nothing at all,
They can have that advice for free.

I'm aware it's my decision to watch them enact
Their ridiculous display of dumb babble.
But just maybe one day, they'll just come out,
With a word that scores more than 20 in Scrabble.

* * *

TIME FLIES

As the year comes to an end, people often remark,
That they can't believe how quickly it has passed.
Weeks became months within a blink of an eye,
Old age is creeping up on us so fast.

They say that 'time flies when you're having fun',
And it drags at a snail's pace when you are not.
So maybe you should do something boring and dull,
Where days will crawl by when doing diddly squat.

Watch an egg boil in a large saucepan of water,
Or stare at your washing machine's final spin.
Perhaps observe a potato cooking in a microwave,
Standing alone, glaring, perhaps even sipping at gin.

The combination of boredom and encroaching drunkenness,
Will appear like you've added hours to your day.
Life will no longer feel like it's passing you by,
You've done much to keep the quickening time at bay.

Waiting for the weekend on a Monday morning,
Is another way to ensure the clock slows down.
Or just focusing on a holiday, six months from now,
It will surely replace your smile with a frown.

There's nothing wrong with exciting yourself,
With the notion of a fun, future event.
But it's the here and now, you should target,
And the thrill of an upcoming pleasure will augment.

The alternative is to let time run its course,
To relish whatever life has offered you.
Time spent enjoying yourself is time well spent,
One's period on earth is not just a preview.

Occupy your day; it's what makes life worth living,
Even if it passes by faster than you'd expect,
But failing that, you can always go back to watch,
That slowly boiling egg in while you reflect.

* * *

BULB

The bulb had 'gone' for over a week.
And I guessed it was high time to change it.
The shadow formed over half of my lounge
Made the room dark and gloomy, I admit.

From the kitchen cupboard, I fetched a new one,
And back to the wall light above where I was sitti.ng
Only after taking the spent one out,
I realised it was the wrong damn fitting.

Of all the bulbs in all the cupboards,
None of them was the right fit for my light.
So I went on my laptop and from an online store,
And bought half a dozen on that darkening night.

Then a worrying realisation dawned upon me.
Was I sure the fittings I bought were 'screw'?
The bayonet ones had no purpose I could think of.
The numbers in the cupboard, are starting to accrue.

I checked my order; I think the correct bulbs I did buy.
In two or three days, they'd be here, for sure.
And my lounge will be well laminated again
Instead of the half-light, I've recently had to endure.

Two days later, they arrived –
Much sooner than I expected!
I took them out of the well-padded box.
And immediately; a problem, I suspected.

Of course, I ordered the wrong bloody type.
Of course, the size difference is stark.
And of course, the other bulb then failed me too
Leaving me dumbfounded and alone in the dark.

* * *

A FINE TURNOUT

All these people have come to see me,
It's quite a turnout; I have to say.
Family and friends from very near and quite far,
On this beautifully sunny, cloudless day.

Aunts and uncles I haven't seen for years,
So many cousins I never knew I had.
Conversing and smiling amongst one another,
Shaking hands and chatting with my old Dad.

I remember that girl. I haven't seen her in years,
I have to admit she's aged awfully well.
An old girlfriend appears at the back of the crowd,
Ever the dazzling blonde bombshell.

A group of pals I haven't seen since school,
All grown up, wearing suits and ties.
Mutter to each other and fidget uncomfortably,
Looking like Mafia henchmen in unconvincing disguise.

Work colleagues from over the years,
Re-acquaint and recant the odd tale,
About what I did to the area manager one Christmas,
In fine and pinpoint accurate detail.

My next-door neighbours have made the trip,
That's nice of them to turn up today.
Being greeted by my wife and children,
As they all shuffle down the pathway.

It's incredible that such an array of folks,
Have all made an effort to come together.
On this, the most auspicious of days,
All my friends, both good and fairweather.

I wish I could tell them of my appreciation,
All of them - from agnostic to orthodox.
But I can't talk. I shall speak no more,
As I lie still inside this wooden box.

I wish I'd worn my glasses on that fateful day,
Or decided to give porridge oats a miss.
Because out-of-date rat poison with warm milk,
Would be something I would normally dismiss.

* * *

AN EARLY NIGHT

At last! An opportunity for an early night.
The house is empty. They've all gone out.
The kids are at a party and my wife at a hen night,
Leaving me alone. Silence. No one about.

Lying on the couch, I watch the news, then I'll turn in.
I like to be abreast of the news events.
Then again, Match of the Day starts in a few minutes.
But my team lost, and I don't want to get uptight and tense.

It's no good; I'm just not sleepy anymore.
Just typical. If i'd watched the TV, I'd be tired alright.
A milky drink and a bit of a read might work,
Although it's now getting close to midnight.

I did promise myself I'd finish the chapter,
Of the thriller novel I've just started to read.
It's hardly very thrilling or gripping in any way,
That's why I've been paused on page 20, unable to proceed.

My eyes crawled to page 11, and that was an effort,
I think the author should try writing in a different style.
Maybe a self-help book- *How to Bore People to Sleep*,
It would be better than reading this lot of old bile.

I switch off the light, only to be alerted by another.
The blue flashing warning from my mobile phone.
I check the latest ramblings on Facebook and Whatsapp.
And Twitter… and then my emails. Tik Tok, I'll postpone

Finally, darkness joins the silence, as I ready myself for sleep,
I rest my head on my pillow and close my eyes.
"Did I leave the door 'unlocked'? Now, there's a juxtaposition.
I best check it, or my wife and kids will get a surprise.

Of course, I did. As if I'd lock them out.
I trundle back upstairs and get back into bed.
I resume the same position, but it's not the same,
Fidgeting and squirming, I try several others instead.

I switch the bedside lamp and stare at the ceiling,
My eyes wide open, I let out a sigh in despair.
I watch a spider drop towards me on a thin thread of silk,
How can I possibly go to sleep now? I wouldn't dare.

So I cup the arachnid and drop him out of the window,
I lookout. The street is so peaceful and quiet now.
I wonder how many neighbours are in the land of nod?
Huh! So much for my broken 'early night' vow.

A key in the door and the sound of booze-induced laughter.
Signifies the final death knell of my early night.
It's almost one o'clock, and the house is alive,
It was never going to happen, I realise in hindsight.

So much for a rare early night,
Next time I'm alone, I won't even try,
I'll do something useful or go out myself,
Even if it's just down the pub or somewhere nearby.

* * *

CELEBRITY

A celebrity used to be a somebody-
A huge star of song, stage or screen.
Nowadays, though, to the detriment of all,
They can be just any desperate old has been.

Whether you're in demand to feature,
In a massive new Hollywood blockbuster,
Or a washed-up old actor, fading away,
And who's long since lost their lustre.

Any blogger, vlogger or non-league clogger,
Can now become a household name.
They just have a rant on social media,
And worldwide fame they can claim.

Maybe you can completely butcher,
A song and put it up online.
And with a Christmas number one under your belt,
Your 'talent' will surely shine.

In recent years, a housemate on Big Brother,
Is regularly lauded and rewarded,
With gigs opening supermarkets,
And all the adoration that that afforded.

Maybe they'll get an appearance
Sitting on the sofa on GMTV.
To promote a tell-all expose,
On what the viewers didn't see.

Years ago, you had to do something special,
And dedicate your life to your trade.
As a musician, an actor or a TV presenter,
You had to work hard to make the grade.

To be a somebody; a talent to inspire,
And for the right reasons, make the news.
Not just someone whose drunken YouTube video,
Clicks up five or six million views.

Don't get me wrong; it's certainly not only,
The fame-seeking individuals I blame.
They're just the ones who are so desperate,
To find Warhol's 15 minutes of fame.

It's the followers, fans and disciples,
Of these random, lucky, non-entities,
Who can't even begin to get enough
Of their new idol's newly-created identities.

Why does the public, in their finite wisdom,
Lap up this made-up fame?
And also, why do they give these 'celebrities'
So much damn acclaim?

Is it because that, by association,
They long to feel the touch,
Of the unattainable Z-list lifestyle,
That they crave so very much.

* * *

ROLLING NEWS... ROLLING NEWS... ROLLING NEWS...

'If I told you once, I told you a thousand times'-
-The parental admonishment that is most fitting.
To the never-ending wave of rolling TV news.
Due to the remote disappearing from where I am sitting.

BREAKING NEWS!! that "broke" an hour ago,
Rolls across the screen on an endless ribbon of red.
I have to say that even when it broke, it was not "new",
I heard the story on the radio this morning when still in bed.

But it keeps on rolling along, drawing the eye.
Maybe someone somewhere is still unaware,
That the woman married to the sixth in line to the throne,
Is pregnant again, and perhaps they even care.

I'm other news; the Prime Minister's making a speech in Belgium.
I know. I've been shown that seven times in 20 minutes.
His tie has thirteen diagonal green stripes on a blue background.
I didn't count his stutters. My OCD does have its limits.

The weather is set fine with a high temperature of 8 degrees.
The same as it was about five minutes ago.
Although in the Northwest, it has started to rain.
So much for the imminent dire threat of snow.

Unemployment figures are up, and The FTSE is down,
And so is the curtain on a new London musical show.
Any shits I gave when I first heard this news,
Were lost near the beginning of this constant flow.

Its midday and time for a change of presenters,
The top of the hour welcomes a fresh crew.
But will they bring with them something new to report on?
No, there's Boris still wearing that tie, 13 green stripes on blue.

It's no good. I need to find the remote and quickly.
This ever-repeating non-news is driving me barmy.
Of course, I was sitting on it. Now, what else is on?
Ah, the four millionth repeat of Dad's Army.

* * *

STAG NIGHT FAIL

'Welcome to your last night of freedom,'
My best man, Frank, chuckled with delight.
Struggling to handcuff me to a parking meter,
I thought it best not to put up too much of a fight.

The irony of his statement was not lost,
But I had to warn the "not very bright spark."
'Surely this should be your coup de grace
It's only 7.30 pm, and it's not even dark.'

He saw my point, and I was released,
And we walked to our first port of call.
To meet up with the rest of my stag party group,
Outside the entrance of the old shopping mall.

The waiting posse numbered just three,
For an age, we waited for the rest to arrive.
A true pointer to the esteem they hold me in,
Was the complexity of the excuses they chose to contrive.

The "not so" magnificent seven were hungry
And were all very keen on being fed.
So, to the other side of town, we began our stroll.
Why didn't we meet up there instead?"

Concluding our walk through the winter cold,
We bundled into the curry house at last.
Poppadums, chutney and lager were ordered,
Before 20 seconds had even passed.

An hour later, we were one man short,
An ambitious vindaloo accounted for Jay.
Not that mattered all that much to me,
As he wasn't actually invited anyway.

Another round of beers was delivered,
When a second member of the party bailed out.
A phone call from Phil's wife, who had taken ill.
We were down to six, and the evening was now in doubt.

'We collect the tickets at the door of the club?'
'We do, and we have a private booth to boot,' said Rab.
'Nice one," I replied with a mouthful of Dhansak,
And at this rate, we'd all fit into a single cab.'

That would soon become a distinct possibility,
With a loud beep of Rab's mobile phone.
'So sorry, the alarm's gone off in my shop.
I'm going to have to leave you five guys alone.'

Then Dan went to the loo and didn't return.
His disappearance meant that five became four.
George went in to confirm whereabouts.
It seemed that he legged it through the back door.

'Let's settle up and get out of here,' snorted Frank.
'Before someone else finds an excuse not to stay.'
We asked for the bill and pooled our money
Except for Dan, who'd already scarpered away

We were barely out of the door when George's phone rang,
'What, Mum? You fell down the stairs? I'm on my way.'
He shrugged his shoulders, and I wished him luck.
I mean, what could the poor bugger say?

'We may as well call it a night,' I sombrely suggested.
As we watched a tramp at the bus stop have a pee.
Go on, Dave, you might as well go home too.
My stag do at the nightclub was not to be.

Dave forlornly nodded and walked off into the shadows,
I shook my head, turned to Frank and said,
"As it began, so has it ended, old mate.
I reckon it's best I go home to bed."

'But I still have these; I need to take a snap.'
He pulled the handcuffs from his pocket once more.
'Alright, slap them on, take a photo and free me.'
Why he was obsessed with my confinement, I wasn't sure.

We walked a few yards and stopped abruptly.
'I'll cuff you to this wooden seat here, I think.'
Under the bench was a freshly laid dog poo
'Hurry up and take your picture; this don't half stink.'

Half an hour later, I was at home alone, at last,
And I sat quietly on the edge of my bed.
If this evening was an omen for my future married life,
Then, I think I'd be better off dead.

* * *

A GENUINE SICKIE

I really do feel ill this morning. No word of a lie.
My phone is in my hand. My work number had been entered.
It's the third time in a fortnight. The second this week.
The last time it was sort of true. The first, not so much.
What should I tell them? How should I sound?
I could hold my nose. I could squeeze my gullet.
But that won't convey sickness. However, it might make me vomit.
I can't get out of bed. I feel light-headed and faint.
But I daren't tell them that. It puts out the wrong message.
Like I've had too much to drink. Or eaten a dodgy shrimp.
Alcohol or food poisoning are no-nos. The two worst excuses.
But I genuinely feel rough. I just can't go in to work.
Just a 10-second phone call. They'll understand.
Yeah, sure they will. They'll think immediately it's a put-on.
But it really isn't. Not on this occasion.
Damn! I wish I hadn't lied the first time. I just fancied a day off
And the toothache on Monday was gone by half nine.
They'll assume I'm lying. But this time, it's genuine
But how can I convince them? What should I say?
My finger hovers over the call button. And then I withdraw.

I'm going to have to be brave. I'll go to work after all.
Then they'll see how I'll I am. They'll tell me to go home.
Who am I kidding? I'll have to feign a collapse to stand a chance.
So that is what I'll do. Who needs dignity, anyway?
I'll vomit on my computer. I'll faint and drop to the floor.
This is what I've been reduced to. Damn those disbelieving swines.
But what am I going to do next Wednesday? A midnight stag night -
why?
A broken wrist? A death in the family? The kids are ill?
Perhaps, I'll just quit my job. It's hardly worth all this bother.
Then I can be as sick as I like. And for as often as I like.

* * *

WHAT HAVE I GOT TO LOSE?

'Go on. Do it! What have you got to lose?'
It's a common little cliché men like to explore.
But beware, it's a dare, a challenge, a provocation,
And the answer might be–*everything* and more.

Asked by someone who might wish you to fall.
And who wouldn't, themselves, ever take a chance.
They might want you to bomb, crash and burn.
Which might result in their fortunate advance.

Let's begin with our old friend, money,
And being asked loan, invest or bet.
If a fool and his money are easily parted,
Will you be the fool who'll soon regret?

Reputation is something that cannot be bought,
But it can be easily lost in a trice.
Years to build and a moment to lose,
On a coin toss or roll of a dice.

How about your wife, your girlfriend, or both?
Your children, your house or your job?
Or perhaps your looks, your teeth and straight nose,
Just to fight someone for a few bob.

Respect is another thing you can fritter away,
Because you acted too quickly, in haste.
And let's not forget your honour and dignity,
Lost, all because your trust was misplaced.

Some things you can never retrieve,
Just by agreeing; to look like a boss.
So think on and think clear before you act,
Does the gain outweigh the loss?

So if someone asks, 'What have you got to lose?'
'Everything,' could be the answer to confide.
Because there's invariably something to be lost,
Even if it's just your sense of male pride.

* * *

INDIAN SUMMER

'We're in for an Indian Summer,'
The weather forecasters have had their say.
Like they do pretty much every year,
To try and stifle the country's dismay.

When the end of August is a washout,
News of any warm spell brings late joy.
The hope of one more weekend barbeque,
And a slathering of sunscreen to deploy.

From Bangalore, Chennai, and Mumbai,
To Basingstoke, Cheshunt, and Maidstone.
The arrival of the hot sub-continental sun,
Does its best to set the early autumn tone.

Every year it's the same old thing,
Until August Bank Holiday, conditions are cool.
The drop in temperature is guaranteed.
Right up until the kids go back to school.

Why they even call June, "summer" is a joke,
Especially as April showers come in May.
We should move the seasons on a month,
That should keep the summer drizzle at bay.

So just when the holidays are over,
The sun then sneaks out to play.
'I've been here all the time, just hiding,'
Transforming the skies blue from slate grey.

I wonder what happens in India -
Is a 'British summer' something over there?
Does Hyderabad get drenched in warm rain?
And does sleet in Goa cause local despair?

Of course, our Indian Summer may not last,
It might only be present for a day or two.
But that doesn't prevent weather forecasters,
Spreading hope, which will inevitably fall through.

* * *

LOVE IS A RED SWEET

You can eat your last Rolo if you want,
I know the one who truly loves me.
She's the one who offers her last red fruit pastille,
And to get it, I never have to ask or plea.

That goes for a packet of Starburst too,
Or Opal Fruits as they should still be known.
The last strawberry sweet my love will save for me,
Better than 100 lime chews, which I can't condone.

And if a packet of wine gums were purchased,
The remaining red one will be given with affection.
Because eating the yellow and green gums herself,
Is the best way to show a genuine love connection.

It's easy to offer up your final Rolo,
As a tube holds a dozen chocolates or more.
But saving a last solitary red confection,
Is to prove her true love for me, evermore.

* * *

WHAT'S THERE TO WRITE ABOUT?

Sometimes it's tough to know what to write,
When you think you've covered every subject.
From getting into trouble in primary school
To seeing old pals, hoping to reconnect.

Holidays, birthdays and family occasions,
Have all been remembered in rhyming verse.
Dodgy haircuts, unwanted presents, television,
And dear friends' weddings, for better or worse.

Yesterday I was in full poetic flow,
Ideas and words simply shot into my head.
But just 24 hours and one long sleep later,
It's writer's block - the thing I most dread.

I look out of the windows of my lounge,
But I see nothing to give me any inspiration.
A few parked cars and a magpie perched on my wall,
Can do nothing to provide me with some cogitation.

Retro sweets, computer games and football stickers,
I've written poems about all those things over time.
Because everyone loves a bit of old skool nostalgia,
Especially when their beloved memories rhyme.

Phone scammers, roadworks and late post,
Have all been deserved recipients of my wrath.
In poetic terms, in any event,
Although they all really do cheese me off.

Cinemas, theatres, libraries and parks,
Have all been central subjects of my writing.
So they're off-limits to any new written piece.
I need to find something else for highlighting.

I've created poems on driving and taking the tube,
Travelling on a bus, a boat and even a plane.
Clearing out the crap in the attic and my garage,
Written with the help of memories I retain.

My kids and my aspirations for their future,
Deep, hidden memories and all that lies in the past.
What more is there for me to write about?
The bright outlook of yesterday is now somewhat overcast.

I know! I can write about everything I've already written.
All those nostalgic memories and the observations.
Hold on; I think I've just completed that very thing,
And created a poem with those exact foundations.

* * *

115

About the Author

Can It Still Just Be Me? is Elliot Stanton's eighth book and his third book of poetry, following, *It Can't Just Be Me* and *Can It Be Just Me?* Four of his previous books are humorous novels that all have various aspects of true-life events, but he decided he wanted to try something different this time. So, in the spring of 2019, he decided to write a series of Tales of the Unexpected–type stories and 12 months later, he'd written enough tales to create *The Crimson Scarf and Other Short Stories*. During the pandemic lockdown in early 2021, he started writing short, humorous poems on the things seen and experienced. They culminated in three collections of poetry, of which this is the final one.

His interests include history, watching sport, music and travel. His favourite location is Las Vegas, where he has visited many times. In fact, Vegas is the location of his second novel, *For A Few Dollars Less.*

If you've enjoyed reading this book, please leave him a review on Amazon. https://www.amazon.co.uk/dp/B09TMTCP1Z

You can connect with me on:

🌐 https://www.elliotstanton.com

🐦 https://twitter.com/elboy44

📘 https://www.facebook.com/groups/1561342593910186

Also by Elliot Stanton

Available on Amazon as paperbacks and downloads or visit Elliot's website at https://www.elliotstanton.com

Can It Be Just Me?
In life, there is a myriad of situations that can leave us happy and refreshed or simply baffled. There are nice things like waking up on a warm, sunny Sunday morning with nothing else to do apart from figuring out our place in the world. And then there are annoying things like never-ending roadworks, losing wallets and keys, or receiving swathes of junk mail. Humour can be found in most situations- even if we can't necessarily find it immediately.

Presents From The Past

We all love a bit of nostalgia, and even unfortunate or infuriating events can become fond and well-loved memories over time. Presents From The Past is a humour-infused collection of fifty poems that I have created from such memories. Many of them are from childhood and have lived long in my consciousness, but some are a little more recent and have only just laid down roots in my mind.

This book features poetic reminiscences of such subjects as favourite bygone snacks and old TV programmes, the thrill of the last day of school and attending your first football match, teenage trips to the local cinema and memories of treasured family vacations.

Every reader will find something that resonates deeply, thus providing that warm, satisfying glow of nostalgia we often long for.

The Crimson Scarf and Other Stories

A collection of 17 short stories that will satisfy the imaginations of those who enjoy fiction with entertaining and unexpected twists.

In life, you don't always get a 'happy ever after', no matter how hard you wish. Not every mystery can be solved, and occasionally the bad guy wins. While Karma dictates that wrongdoers get their comeuppance, and 'what goes around, comes around', this is not always the case. Occasionally, what comes around has been around and gone elsewhere.

Some people are good: others do things for the right reason, but end up doing more bad than good; some set out to harm, but finally find a conscience and a few are evil through and through. The characters within *The Crimson Scarf and Other Stories* are diverse, and for many of them, the consequences of their actions do not always acknowledge the rules of Karma.

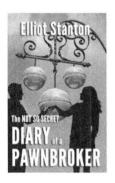

The Not So Secret Diary of a Pawnbroker

Middle-aged, married man with three grown-up children, Pete Dawson, an East London pawnbroker, finds himself living a predictable and quite often, boring life. Over time, an opportunity for change arises when his young, female work colleague takes an interest in him. it is a feeling which becomes mutual.

However, Pete starts to realise that something is not quite as it should be…

For a Few Dollars Less

A stag trip to Las Vegas doesn't go quite to plan. A nightclub fracas, a street altercation featuring film and TV 'stars' is just the beginning. When things escalate to arms smuggling, a suspected homicide and a Mafia double-crossing, the members of The Syndicate soon realise that their vacation to Sin City was not what any of them expected.

Questionable Friends

They say it's not *what* you know, it's *who* you know. But, what happens when you find out that you don't know these people as well as you thought?

The journey from the sticky beer-stained tables of their local pub, to the slick, pristine studio set of a nationwide television quiz programme is swift. However, for Mike Knight and his team of quizzers, events unfold that change all of their lives.

To coin a phrase - Keep your friends close, and your fellow quiz teammates even closer.

The Not So Secret Diary of a Store Detective

Five years have passed since the events of *The Not So Secret Diary of a Pawnbroker* and recently divorced Pete Dawson begins work as a supermarket store detective. Matters outside his control continue to concern him; none greater than the actions of the incumbent U.S. President and the closure of his local Chinese takeaway. However a chance meeting with an enticing ghost from his past gives him much to ponder.

The Not So Secret Diary of a Store Detective is an amusing and entertaining insight into the life of a worried man whose mid-life crisis is happening right before his very eyes.

Printed in Great Britain
by Amazon

82975892R00078